THROUGH A NEEDLE'S EYE

Luke 18:18-27, FOR CHILDREN

Written by Muriel Hemmings
Illustrated by Betty Wind

ARCH Books

Copyright © 1979 Concordia Publishing House, St. Louis, Missouri
MANUFACTURED IN THE UNITED STATES OF AMERICA
ALL RIGHTS RESERVED
ISBN 0-570-06125-3

A long line of camels
Tramped wearily forth
On Judea's roadway
From Tyre, in the north.

Each camel was carrying
Sacks that were full
Of shiny gold dishes
And fine, purple wool.

3

The leader called, "Hurry
With all of your might.
We must reach Jerusalem
Before it is night."

4

The very last camel
Held Amos, the son
Of proud, wealthy parents.
He traveled "for fun."

Away from his folks
In this land strange and new
No person was going to
Tell HIM what to do.

So Amos kept lagging
Still farther behind,
Exploring all rivers
And caves he could find.

To a small group of men
His attention was drawn,
Then to one special Person
Whose face fairly shone,

Whose eyes were so tender,
Whose smile showed His love.
"This Man must be Jesus
From heaven above!

"My friends all have wished
This great Man they could see.
Just wait till I tell them
What's happened to me!"

And Amos heard this:

A rich man asked Jesus,
"How can I get to Heaven?"

"Come follow Me, and
Give up all you've been given."

Amos watched the rich man,
Who glittered with gold.
Amos saw he was saddened
By what he'd been told.

14

The Savior stood mournfully
Shaking His head,
Saw Amos' camel
And here's what He said:

"IT IS EASIER FOR A CAMEL
TO GO THROUGH A NEEDLE'S EYE
THAN FOR A RICH MAN TO ENTER
INTO THE KINGDOM OF GOD."

Amos thought later,
As his camel trudged on,
"For me will all hope of
Sweet heaven be gone?"

He knew it was easier
For donkeys to fly
Than to push a big camel
Through a small needle's eye.

Must he give away toys
And fine clothes to be sure
He'd end up in heaven?
Did he HAVE to be poor?

He said, "YES! I'D DO IT."

The next thing he knew
The sun had gone down
And the sky was deep blue.

The rest of the camels
Were nowhere in sight.
The gates of Jerusalem
Were locked for the night!

Poor Amos was frightened.
Now where could he go?
He scolded his camel
For being so slow.

He thought about robbers
And could not forget
His stomach was empty
With no supper yet.

He then noticed something
He'd not seen before.
At the side of the gates
Stood a tiny-sized door.

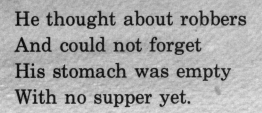

But there stood his camel
So big and so tall.
It never could go through
A doorway that small.

Or could it? Well, first
Amos took off the load.
He then had his camel
Kneel down on the road.

It bowed its head low,
And Amos turned blue
Struggling and pushing,
But it couldn't go through.

A miracle happened!
Big gates opened wide!
The keeper in pity
Let Amos inside.

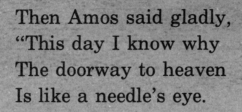

Then Amos said gladly,
"This day I know why
The doorway to heaven
Is like a needle's eye.

"Though we drop every burden
That keeps us away
And bow and kneel humbly
To Jesus and pray,

"We need something more
To pass through heaven's door:
God's love and forgiveness
For life evermore."

DEAR PARENTS:

When the rich man discovered he would need to sell all his possessions and give the proceeds to the poor in order to follow Jesus, he was sad. He was not able to do this, for he loved his wealth too much, and he could not serve God and mammon. It was at this point that Jesus says: "It is easier for a camel to go through the eye of a needle than for a rich man to enter the kingdom of God." The disciples reply is the obvious one, "Who then can be saved," for we all love the things of this life too much. Jesus' reply is the salvation message: What is impossible for men is possible for God.

Amos, of course, is a fictional character, but through him the story becomes clearer to our children. It is impossible for us to enter heaven on our own. We need Jesus Christ and the salvation he offers. Heaven is possible for us through Him.

Read the complete story in Luke 18:18-27 with your children, then read the story *Through a Needle's Eye* a second time, emphasizing especially the last two verses, to be sure your children understand the story message.

THE EDITOR